ADULT HUNT

Book 2 Holodeck Maze Games

DR. ROSELINDA JOHNSON, ED.D.

authorHOUSE®

AuthorHouse™
1663 Liberty Drive
Bloomington, IN 47403
www.authorhouse.com
Phone: 1 (800) 839-8640

Published by AuthorHouse   07/13/2015

ISBN: 978-1-5049-1954-8 (sc)
ISBN: 978-1-5049-1953-1 (e)

Print information available on the last page.

Any people depicted in stock imagery provided by Thinkstock are models, and such images are being used for illustrative purposes only. Certain stock imagery © Thinkstock.

This book is printed on acid-free paper.

ADULT HUNT 2

Finally, all the 50 contestants and their parents had arrived and were in their appointed room assignments. I am sure that all the technical equipment and luxury of their surroundings impressed them all. The parents did not know what was in store for them because they were not given all the information that the contestants were given.

After the time for the Holodeck Maze Games had begun, all the contestants were fed and clothed in their new outfits and were sitting in front of their TV screens awaiting news of what would happen next and what was expected of them. The parents, on the other hand, didn't have a clue of what was going to happen to them next. I am certain that their anxiety levels were off the charts. Some of them probably were even scared of the future events.

The only thing that alarmed both the contestants and the parents was the realization that the angel rings that they had on their fingers could not be removed no matter how hard they tried to take the rings off. Also, the contestants were informed that they could create their own games if they did not like any of the games already programmed into the computer for the Holodeck Maze Game. They were also informed that they could forgive their abusers and eliminate all the games.

The people in charge had arranged for a giant, glass bubble to be placed in the middle of the downstairs entry hall that was full of the fifty numbers that had been previously assigned to each pair of contestants and parents. Once everyone was situated in their rooms, the numbers began to float upward toward a receptacle which then sent the number selected to the main control room. When the first number was selected in this random fashion, the control room notified the contestant and the parent by turning the eyes of the angel ring to change colors to ruby red. The door was automatically unlocked and they walked to their predetermined Holodeck Maze for the game to begin. The parent entered a door with the title, "Parable of the Net", while the child entered another door with the title, "Parable of the Mustard Seed".

The first number drawn was 7. His name was Robin from Hartford, Connecticut. His parents made him sleep on the floor in the hall. As he looked over his choices for the game, he chose to create his own game. It was called "Dinosaurs". His parent was sent back to the past when the dinosaurs ruled the earth and man had not shown up yet. He was given only a spear to protect himself and no food. He was attacked immediately by a Tyrannosaurs Rex. He had to hide in a cave that was nearby and sleep on the floor of the cave with only leaves to keep him warm. He managed to find some water in a nearby stream and ate some red berries that grew beside the cave. The next day, he speared a small mammal, but had no fire to cook it so he had to eat it raw. By now, he felt sick because the berries he had eaten were poison. He lay on the floor of the cave and curled up in a fetal position and wished that he were home. The floor of the cave was as hard as the floor that he had made his son sleep on. He cried out that he was sorry and asked his son to forgive him. Immediately, his ring turned from ruby red to emerald green, and he was released from the game. His son was watching all this on his TV and forgave his father. They both returned to their rooms.

The next number drawn was 18. Her name was Pelican from Baton Rouge, Louisiana. Her mother had forced her to binge drink vodka until she passed out. Then the mother invited her gay friends to play out their sexual fantasies on her body. Pelican chose a new game that she selected from the computer called "Detox". The mother entered the door and was immediately put into a strait jacket and taken to a padded cell where she was not allowed anything to drink. As time sped up in the game, it took her 4 weeks to detox from all of her alcohol consumption. She screamed in pain, vomited, and had hallucinations of being raped by groups of people that wouldn't stop until she passed out. Once she was sober, she was released from her strait jacket and allowed to drink some health shakes and shower. She still showed no remorse so her angel ring was still ruby red. Pelican then chose another game that her mother had to enter.

This game was called "Buried Alive". The mother was placed in a steel coffin and buried in the ground. She yelled and yelled until she ran out of oxygen, then she passed out. The daughter took pity on her mother and quickly chose Game 9," Forgiveness" and let her mother get out of the coffin and leave the Holodeck Maze Game. The mother was so relieved that she asked her daughter to forgive her and said she would never abuse her again. With that statement, the mother's angel ring turned to emerald green. Both of them returned to their respective rooms where they ate a wonderful meal, showered, and relaxed in the hot tubs before going to sleep for the night.

I was glad that I did not have to be first to go through the Holodeck Maze. This would give me time to evaluate which game would best fit my situation. I told Robin that he had made a good game choice, and that I was happy his father had shown remorse so quickly. I also called Pelican and told her that her mother had come a long way to obtain forgiveness. I wish I could call my boyfriend and share all that is happening, but we are not allowed any outside contact. I turned off my TV, ate dinner, and went to sleep.

When I awoke, I turned on the TV to see who had been chosen next. It was Magnolia, Contestant 24 who had been raped by a stranger. Her parents had shown no signs of compassion and told her it had been her fault. She chose to have her mother go through a game that she had chosen called "Alien Abduction" where the mother would be transported to an alien ship where she would be examined by doctors who would experiment on her. The mother walked into the area, Parable of the Net, and the child took over the Holodeck Maze Game controls in the area, Parable of the Mustard Seed. The mother was already angry that she had to go through the holodeck maze game and was not prepared for what her child had in store for her. The mother was given a drug to make her feel pain more intensely. She was instantly grabbed by a large, grey alien who immediately teleported her to his ship. The table that she was strapped to was made of cold steel with sensors attached to her body. She was given a probe that tested her fertility and emitted a foreign reproductive organ that attached itself to her womb. The length of time from fertilization to delivery was only one hour so before she knew it, she was giving birth to a foreign organism. Her labor was painful and long. The aliens took the newly delivered organism and put it into an incubator. It was long and red with green eyes. It had feathers and a long tail. The only sound she heard was a screeching sound that was high and shrill. The aliens let her loose and returned her to the original room she had entered. She was so afraid that she begged her daughter to forgive her for not believing she had been raped. Magnolia took pity on her mother and released her from the game. They met at the exit and went back to their rooms where they both took a shower and ordered some food. The mother was exhausted from her ordeal. Her angel ring's eyes turned green and she fell into a deep sleep.

I awoke the next morning and ate a cheese omelet with toast and coffee. I was anxious to see who the next contestant would be. I turned on my TV to await the posting of the next numbers. Suddenly there it was number 41. Her code name was Pheasant. Her mother had cut off all her hair and her nails down to the quick. The mother and contestant met at the 2 doorways and didn't say a word to each other. Pheasant looked over all the games and decided to create her own holodeck maze game especially designed for her mother. The game began with the mother being stripped of all her clothes and a leather body harness was attached to her body. There was a purple cylinder filled with a liquid that would remove all the hair on her body. She gaged on the liquid, but there was nothing she could do until Pheasant created the next part of the game. Slowly, the body harness lifted her out of the liquid which had dyed her skin a dark purple. Two men in white coats placed her on an operating table where they strapped her down and proceeded to pull out all her finger and toe nails which bled profusely. She screamed, but they showed her no mercy. She was then put onto a pulley that lifted her up in the air onto another platform where she was washed and scrubbed with SOS steel pads and powdered with a salt solution that stung her body and left her wet while they then toweled her off and hung her upside down to dry off. The ring on her finger flickered from red to green so her daughter stopped the game and released her to return to her room where she took a bath and went to sleep. The daughter got to go get her own hair washed and combed into a beautiful style as it was growing out fast. She was given a manicure and pedicure that made her hands and feet look beautiful. Pheasant's green eyes were happy at last as she returned to her room for the night.

I went to my kitchen and prepared a snack by using my 3-D printer. I told it to create a hamburger and chocolate milk shake. It only took it 10 minutes, and my snack was delicious. I took a hot shower and went to bed. While I was going to sleep, I wondered who would be chosen for the next day's Holodeck Maze Game. When I woke up, I turned on the TV to see what numbers had been randomly chosen. The number 50 rolled into view which meant that Paintbrush and the minister who had raped him had been picked.

Paintbrush and the minister at his church walked into the Holodeck Maze. Paintbrush didn't like any of the games that were offered because they were not severe enough to make up for all the suffering that the minister had caused him. The minister was transported to his old congregation where he was tied to a cross and made to tell of the many abuses he had caused. The congregation told him that he could never come back to their church again and voted to have him castrated for raping Paintbrush and several other altar boys. The Deacons carried out the procedure without giving him any anesthetic for his pain and cut off his private parts and put them in an offering plate on the altar of the church. He cried for mercy, but his angel ring had not yet turned green showing that he still felt no remorse. Then the Deacons heated up a branding iron with a cross on it and burned the symbol onto his body until the minister blacked out. Paintbrush did not take pity on him so the torture continued. The minister was taken down from the cross and carried to the baptismal font where he was held under the water until he died. Paintbrush told the Deacons to resuscitate him and to carry him to the main altar where he was tied down with his vestment shawls and made to announce all the names of the boys that he had abused and raped over the 10 years he had been at the church. As their names were called out, each abused boy was allowed to do whatever they wanted to him. Some cut off his fingers and toes. Some cut off his ears and nose. Others gauged out his eyes and cut off his tongue. Finally, the minister's angel ring changed from red to emerald green which indicated that he was remorseful for his past actions. He was untied and taken back to the original Holodeck Maze Chamber where all of his wounds were healed. Then he walked out to the back door and left the arena a changed man. Paintbrush felt that all the minister's suffering had cleared the slate for the many abuses so he went back to his own room and felt that he had finally gotten closure over the rape he had suffered.

The next day I woke up feeling refreshed and hoped that my number would be chosen. I ate a large breakfast, showered, and sat down in front of the TV waiting for the announcement of the next numbers to be announced. The number that flashed across the screen was 19. The contestant's code name was Chickadee. Her mother had put stainless steel wire bands on her fingers to make her stop biting her nails down to the quick. She had been so nervous that she started pulling her hair out by the handfuls so her mother shaved all her hair off.

Chickadee and her mother's rings turned red so their doors were automatically unlocked and they went into the Holodeck Maze Chamber. Chickadee created her own game by having her mother's whole body encased in sharp, stainless steel wires. She then released thousands of biting bugs that flew around her mother and stung her. The mother was immobilized and could not get the bugs off her body as they bite her again and again. Her skin was red and swollen to the point that the sharp wires cut into her flesh and blood started pouring out of the cuts. Her mother asked her for help, but Chickadee would not stop the game because her mother's ring had not turned to green yet to show remorse. Chickadee added vampire bats to attack her mother and they started sucking the blood from her body. Her mother screamed and passed out. Chickadee realized that her mother needed help so she stopped the game by removing all the bugs and bats and lowering her mother to a soothing bath that healed all the wounds and melted the steel wires. When the mother regained consciousness, she silently thanked her daughter and said she was sorry. Her ring turned green, and she was allowed to walk out of the Holodeck Maze Chamber. He daughter hugged her and told her that all was forgiven, and they went back to their rooms.

I went swimming in my pool, washed my hair, and turned on the TV for the morning announcement about the next number to be drawn. After a while, the number that was retrieved from the machine was number 26. Her code name was Montana. Her father had thrown things at her for stuttering. He had not taken her to a speech therapist yet and only made fun of her. The both walked into the Holodeck Maze Game. Montana chose to create her own game. The father was strapped to an operating table where he was not allowed to move while the doctors cut his tongue off. He was then released and made to talk into a phone to ask his daughter to forgive him. He could not speak but only made a rattling sound without a tongue. Each time he would try to speak, large swinging steel balls would zoom past his head. He would try to dodge them, but they were too big. He was hit several times for not being able to speak clearly. Finally, his ring turned green. His daughter let him leave the Maze at which time his tongue was reattached, and he could talk. They both left the area and returned to their rooms. He told Montana that he would never make fun of her stuttering again.

I loved the way the abusers show remorse and leave the Holodeck Maze feeling grateful to their child for allowing them to survive and leave the Maze intact. I turned on the TV to see the next number chosen. The number 29 rolled out of the bubble machine. The name of the contestant was Finch. She was forced to stand outside in the cold when she disobeyed. As the two contestants walked toward the Holodeck Maze

Game, the father asked his child to please try to choose a game that he could survive. Finch created her own game. The father was transported to the North Pole, stripped of his clothes, and dropped down an ice shoot that placed him into an ice cubical where he was frozen into a square chunk of ice. He was then sent to the bottom of the ocean where he was chipped away by luminescent fish that had hot electric tentacles. If he could not escape quickly, he would implode into a thousand pieces. The ring on his finger turned green, and the game ended immediately. The two contestants returned to their respective rooms. The father was glad that his ordeal was over and vowed never to make Finch stand out in the cold again.

Some of the Holodeck Maze Games that the contestants create are much worse than the Maze Games already prepared by the computer. I looked at the new number chosen and saw that it was number 6. Lark's abuser was her father who would play spin the bottle when his friends came over and chose what they would do to sexually molest her. I could only imagine how awful the Holodeck Maze Game would be that Lark would create. I only hoped that her father would show remorse quickly. As the two walked into the arena, Lark's father had to take off the handcuffs and ankle bracelet that the police had put on him. He knew he was in trouble. Lark chose to create a game where her father was stripped naked and cuffed to a large wooden wheel that could spin around until it stopped on different numbers. Each number had a corresponding punishment written on the board. Lark spun the wheel until the wheel stopped on number 1 where the punishment was stripping of her father's skin and an acid was poured over the wounds. She then spun the wheel again; it stopped on number 6 where the punishment was breaking both legs with a large hammer and tearing the bones out of their sockets. Her father was screaming, but his ring had not yet turned green. Lark spun the wheel again, and it stopped on number 10 where the punishment was surgically removing his intestines and cutting off his private parts. At this point, her father's ring turned green so she released him from the game, and he was returned to the state he was in when he had entered the Holodeck Maze. As they left the game, Lark's father asked for her forgiveness and swore he would never allow anyone to molest or abuse her again.

I felt that Lark's game was very severe but effective. I think that she felt that she had been justified in creating a game that scared her father into submission. I looked at the TV for the announcement of the next number to be drawn. It was number 16. Her name is Meadowlark. She had been given cocaine ever since she was ten and forced to have sex with her father's friends where they tied her to a bed and raped her again and again. This was statutory rape because she was just 16. I could not imagine what Holodeck Maze Game she would create for her father. Both of the contestants went into the different chambers of the Holodeck Maze. Her father had to take off his ankle bracelets and handcuffs that the police had put on him. He was visibly scared to death as he faced the game his daughter had chosen. Meadowlark thought for a long time as she created her game. Her father was placed into a steel cage which included an operating table with doctors surrounding him. They proceeded to change his gender by removing his male parts and replacing them with female parts. After this was done, the cage was removed, and he was marched into a room full of large male specimens that proceeded to sexually rape him again and again. He cried out for mercy, but his ring did not turn green showing remorse. The men in the room gave him different kinds of drugs including cocaine while they tried different sexual positions on him. Finally, his ring turned green, and the game was ended. He was allowed to leave the chamber and meet with his daughter as they returned to their respective rooms. He told her again and again how sorry he was to have abused her all her life and would never allow his friends or himself to abuse her again.

I was exhausted from the previous two games. They were so severe that it made my problems with my own parents seem like nothing in comparison. I woke up the next morning and turned on the TV to see what number would be chosen. I didn't have to wait long. The next number was contestant 21. Her code name was Mayflower. Her mother gave her cans of cat food to eat and had her write a thousand times that she would clean the kitchen every day. The two contestants entered the Holodeck Maze Game, and Mayflower chose to create her own game. Her mother was placed in wooden chair and strapped to the arms and legs of the chair so she could not move. There were cages of different animals around the chair including cats and rats. There was a machine that ground up the animals placed it and pumped the liquid to a long plastic tube which was placed in her mother's mouth. As the fluid was pumped into her mouth, the mother tried to throw up while she gagged on the different ground up animals which included their bones, skin, intestines, and hair. This went on until the mother's angel ring turned green. At that point, she was allowed to exit the Maze and return to her room. She hugged her daughter and told her that she was so sorry for abusing her all those years. Mayflower was gaining back some of the weight she had lost and was looking more well-nourished.

I felt like forgiving my mother and not having her go through the Holodeck Maze Game at all. I got up early as usual to see what contestant would be chosen. The number 28 was picked. Her name was Sagebrush. Her mother had used duct tape to tie her down in her room so she would not be so active. Later, a diagnosis was given. She had ADHD and was given the proper medicine so she could focus on school work better. Sagebrush and her mother entered the Holodeck Maze Game together. The game was created to use duct tape to immobilize her mother while she was given a shot to make her hyperactive. The mother kept trying to get up and run around the room. Finally, she gave up as the shot was changed to medicine to calm her down. Now she understood what her daughter had gone through and her ring turned green. Both of them left the Holodeck Maze arm in arm. They returned to their own rooms.

I hope that my number is drawn soon because all the contestants have created their own games and not used the games that were described before. I got up and turned on the TV to view the next number that was chosen. It was number 25. Her name was Hawthorn. Her mother would burn her back with cigarettes when she would not keep her room clean. She chose to create a game for her mother. As they entered the Holodeck Maze Game, the mother was taken to a room and striped of all her clothes and made to lie down on a table that had hundreds of car cigarette lighters on it. She was strapped to the table as another board was lowered on top of her that had another set of similar car cigarette lighters on it. When the board was in place on top of her mother, she pushed a button that turned on all the electric cigarette lighters on at the same time. Her mother's skin was burned both top and bottom. She screamed in terror and pain and asked for forgiveness and promised never to burn her daughter's back with cigarettes again. Hawthorn saw that her mother's angel ring had turned green so she turned the electric cigarette lighters off. Her mother was released from the table and walked out of the room where she and her daughter left to return to their rooms.

I was glad the day was over and all of the abusive parents had shown remorse after their ordeal in the Holodeck Maze Game. I think that

I will just forgive my mother and not have her go through any of the games when our time comes. The next morning the TV announced that the next number chosen was 8. The contestant's name was Blue Hen. Her mother did not keep food in the house, and she would not give her daughter money to buy her school lunch. As the two contestants entered the Holodeck Maze Game, they hugged each other and the mother's ring turned green. Her mother promised to keep food in the house and provide money for her daughter's school lunch. They were both relieved to not have to enter the Maze and went directly back to their rooms.

The next morning I awoke early and turned on my TV. The number picked was 17. The contestant's name was Cardinal. Her mother had taken away her cell phone and laptop because she had spent too much time on Facebook. Both of the contestants entered the Holodeck Maze Game. Cardinal decided to create her own game. She chose to send her mother to Paris to stay in the best hotel and eat all the fine cuisine possible. The mother was surprised at her daughter's generosity and decided to return the favor by allowing her to keep her cell phone and laptop. Her ring turned green, and both of the contestants left the Holodeck Maze and returned to their respective rooms. The mother thanked her daughter and told her to post her adventure on Facebook.

I was tired of watching all the Holodeck Games so I tried to make some jewelry on my 3D printer. I programmed the computer to make another leopard ring for my other finger. It was gold with sapphire eyes and black pearl spots. It took me around an hour, but the ring was beautiful. I put it on my finger and went to sleep. The next morning, I turned on the TV to see who was selected next. The number 37 was chosen. Her name was Grape, and her mother had threatened her by giving her up for adoption if she did not go to school in spite of her high anxiety and low self-esteem. Both of the contestants went into the Holodeck Maze Game. Grape created her own game to cause her mother anxiety and lower her self-esteem. The mother was suspended in a dark chamber and given a gold key to try to open a door that would allow her to escape. She tried over a hundred doors with the key, but none of them would open. She begged her daughter to help her by giving her at least a clue to find the right door. Finally, Grape had the correct door light up so her mother could escape. The mother's ring turned green. They both left the Holodeck Maze Game and went back to their own rooms. The mother promised that she would never threaten Grape to give her up for adoption.

I wished I could call my boyfriend, but the phones would not allow outside calls. I will try to make a cell phone on my 3 D computer to see if it would allow me to call outside the dome area. I waited an hour for it to be complete, and I dialed his number. It worked. When he answered, I told him about all the new games that the contestants had created. He said he hoped that I would be able to come home soon because he missed him. I told him I would call him every chance I could get. I felt much better after our conversation. I turned on the TV to see who would be chosen next. The contestant number 45 rolled out of the machine. Her name was Thrush. She was made to have an abortion by her mother. She also had developed an infection from the abortion procedure and had to go to the school nurse to make an appointment with a good doctor. She didn't want the abortion, but her boyfriend couldn't help pay for her hospital bills nor give her any child support. She said that if she had to do it over again, she would have had the child then put it up for adoption. Thrush decided to create a game for her mother when they entered the Holodeck Maze. The mother was given the option of killing 100 babies or trying to find parents for them. He mother chose to find suitable parents for each child. She selected the parents from the internet and had to contact each one with a description of each baby. This took many days, but she was successful in making the matches. Her ring turned green, and she was allowed out of the Holodeck Maze. As they were going back to their rooms, her mother apologized for making her daughter have an abortion and not placing the baby in an adoption agency.

The next morning I got up early to check the TV for the next contestants. The number selected was 47. The contestants name was Willow. Her mother made her give her baby up for adoption. She missed her baby but felt he was better off with an adult family who would love him and give him shelter. She was too depressed to be creative by programing a new Holodeck Maze Game. So she just forgave her mother, and they both returned to their respective rooms. When Willow arrived at her room, she found a picture of her baby and a note from the adoptive parents. There was also a bottle for a prescription of anti-depression medication which she took immediately.

I was worried about Willow and hoped she would be able to use the money and house that would be given to her at the end of the games to adopt her baby back and be able to take care of herself and her baby. I went to bed late because I had to get some exercise finished and prepare a healthy smoothie. The next morning I awoke to find that the next contestant chosen was number 49. Her name was Hunt. Her father had beaten her severely for not calling him "Sir". As they both entered the Holodeck Maze Game, she would not make eye contact with her father. She created a game that sent her father back in time to World War 2. He was put in a regiment where he was the lowest level of army recruit. In his boot camp, he had to clean out all the bath rooms using a tooth brush and every time his commanding officer came to check on him, he had to respond, "Sir". The next assignment he was given was to clean out the septic tanks for the whole platoon. When he was through with that, he had to wash down all the barracks and make sure all the beds were made. If he did not respond, "Sir", to his commanding officer, he had to do all his tasks over and over again until he remembered to say, "Sir". Soon his ring turned green showing remorse for his actions toward his daughter, and they left the game to return to their rooms.

The next morning when I turned on the TV, the machine picked the number 30. Her name was Purple. Her parents had tied her to a chair for making bad grades. Purple chose the preprogramed game of "Titanic". Her mother is sent back in time. She wakes up in a bunk and finds herself in poor clothing. She gets out of bed quickly and rushes out of the room. She runs frantically through the hallway looking for another person. She finds a poor old woman and asks her where she is. She tells her, "Why, we are on the Titanic." She questions other people who are on board and tries to tell them that the ship is going to sink, and she is from the future in 2021. No one believes her so she begins a fight, and the security guards places her in hand cuffs and attaches them to a chair. They beat her up until she loses consciousness, and when she wakes up, the ship is sinking. She drags the chair to the upper deck of the ship where she sees the wealthy people receiving life jackets and getting into life boats. She jumps off into the freezing water and her body goes into shock. The water is unbearable cold, and she cannot feel her legs. She tries to yell out to a small rescue boat, but she cannot speak because of the below-freezing water. She sinks into the freezing water and dies. Then she wakes up again on the bunk bed in the room in which she woke up earlier. The same event occurs again and again. Finally the mother's ring turns green, and her daughter stops the game. They leave the Holodeck Maze Game and return to their rooms.

I was happy to see all the positive outcomes of the Holodeck Maze Games which seemed to bond the different contestants to their parents. It is such a shame that they couldn't resolve their conflicts before having to go to such extreme measures, but I guess that sometimes it just takes the abusers a long time to realize what they had done to their children. I went to sleep looking forward to what tomorrow would bring. When I woke up, I immediately turned on the TV to see which number had been chosen. The machine picked number 27. Her name was Western. Her mother had not seen fit to have her eyes tested to see if she needed glasses and had instead chosen to just put her in special education at school. The rings turned red, and the two contestants went into the Maze. Western was so glad to see her mother that she chose to forgive her so they could go back to their rooms.

I thought that forgiveness was the best decision, and I considered it to be what I would choose when my turn came. The next day the machine chose number 38. Her name is Laurel. Her mother had not bothered to get rid of the lice in her hair until the nurse at the school washed her hair with medicated shampoo and ran the lice comb through her wet hair to remove all the little eggs that the lice had laid. When their rings turned red, they went to the Maze. Laurel chose to create her own game which included her mother having to run through a large maze while being chased by giant lice. When the mother could not escape, the lice bite her all over until the mother's ring turned green to show remorse. The game was stopped, and the two contestants returned to their rooms to take a shower and eat some food. The mother said she was so sorry that she had not treated her daughter better by examining her hair when she had been told that Laurel's scalp was itching too much.

I looked in the mirror to be sure that I did not have any lice in my own hair. I didn't find any evidence of any, but I felt that my scalp was itchy now. I washed my hair and went to sleep. The next day I turned on the TV to see which contestant had been chosen. The machine chose the number 32. The contestants name was Rose. He was a boy that his mother made him have sex with all of her friends when they came over for evening cocktails. He caught a STD from this and had to go to his family doctor for an antibiotic. His girlfriend had died in a plane crash two weeks ago. When their rings turned red, the son and mother went to the Holodeck Maze to start the game. Rose chose to create his own game. The mother was put into a room where there were several zombies that had STD germs all over their rotting bodies. They each had sex with the mother until she was contaminated not only with the germs, but she was transformed into a zombie herself. When she looked into a mirror and saw her reflection, it was so gross that her ring turned green. Rose stopped the game, and both of the contestants left the Maze to return to their rooms. The mother showered herself again and again to remove all the imagined germs. I was really freaked out with this game because it was so scary. I went to bed and awaited the next morning.

I woke up and decided to make some beautiful jewelry on my 3-D printer. I chose a bright red ruby stone ring that I was going to wear on my other hand. It only took 2 hours to finish my project. It was in sharp contrast to my angel ring and cheered me up after watching the Zombie Maze Game the day before. Finally, I turned on my TV to see which contestants would be chosen. The number 9 was the girl named Blossom. Her parents would lock her in a dark closet without food for days at a time when she did not finish her homework. Her father had been killed by a great white shark while he was surfing. Blossom and her second mother who had treated her like a personal maid entered the Holodeck Maze Game. Blossom chose Game 6: Hawaiian Vacation since she really had recovered from all the trauma in her life and wanted to try to befriend her step mother. Her mother wakes up in a nice beach house on the shore of Hawaii and walks into the kitchen to see the maids cooking a big breakfast of bacon and eggs with orange juice. She walks down to the surf where she swims out and spots a family of dolphins. After playing with them for a while she lets one of them pull her back to the shore by holding on to its fin. She eats fresh pineapple and takes a nap and then decides to go scuba diving where she sees a group of clown fish. She goes back to her straw hut and eats a steak. Her ring has already turned green because she is so grateful that her step daughter allowed her to have such a good time. Both contestants leave the Maze Game and return to their rooms where they dream of palm trees and surging waves. I was really happy that they both bonded more as mother and daughter.

The next morning I got up early to swim in my pool and exercise on the treadmill. After fixing a good breakfast, I turned on the TV. The machine had picked number 12. Her name is Syringa. Her parents made her get up before dawn to feed all the animals on the family farm. When she did not do her chores, they made her sleep in the barn for a week. Their rings turned red and they entered the Holodeck Maze. Syringa decided to create her own game. She made her mother enter a zoo full of kinds of wild animals. She had to clean out all the cages while the animals were still enclosed in the same space. The lions tried to attack her, and she had to run to the gate to get out. The monkey cage was the hardest to clean because the monkeys kept messing up the cleaned areas as soon as she cleaned them. The monkeys kept throwing all kinds of food at her and chased her into the river that surrounded the area which was full of piranha fish that kept biting her legs until they bled. She then went to the snake cage where a 10 foot python wrapped itself around her body until she couldn't breathe. At this point her ring turned green, and the two contestants left the Holodeck Maze and returned to their respective rooms. The mother apologized to Syringa for all the abuse she had endured while sleeping in the barn. I was glad to see that everything ended well for them.

I was tired of getting up every morning just to see which number would be chosen. I was ready for my mother and me to go to the Holodeck Maze and try to see which game I would choose. After eating a large breakfast and swimming several laps in my pool, I decided to turn on the TV and follow what was happening today. The number chosen was 15. The contestants name was Goldfinch. Her parents had screamed at her all the time and called her fat. She was not allowed to eat anything but a piece of toast in the morning, she was given no money for school lunch, and she was only given a cup of soup for supper. She also had to run on a treadmill for 2 hours and do 100 pushups before she could go to bed. Both of their rings turned red, and they entered the Maze through their separate doors. Goldfinch chose to create her own game. She had her mother run up a 10 story building using treadmills, and when she was finished, she had to slide down a long watery tube which lead to a large bowl of cold chicken soup. Her mother was shivering as she immerged from the bowl of soup and tried to dry off with a towel that was on a chair for her to sit in. When she was dressed, she felt herself gaining weight all over her body. There was a mirror for her to see her reflection, and she looked like she had put on at least 300 pounds. She read a card that was on a table which told her to do 300 pushups, and she would be returned to her original weight. She started doing the pushups, but she couldn't do but 50 of them. She started to cry, and her ring turned green. Goldfinch stopped the Holodeck game and allowed her mother to exit the Maze.

She was so sorry that she had abused her daughter all of those years and asked for forgiveness again and again.

The next morning I wanted to talk to someone so I programed my 3-D printer to create a cell phone so I could call my boyfriend. It took 4 hours, and the results looked like it might work. I dialed his number, but the creators of the Game had blocked all attempts to get enough bars on the phone to make it strong enough to reach a number. I then turned on the TV to see what number was chosen today. It was number 33. The contestant's name was Dogwood. Her mother had burned all her favorite books when she did not finish all the chores that she was assigned to do in her room. As they ring's eyes turned red, the proceeded to the Holodeck Maze Game. Dogwood chose to create her own game. She put her mother in a deep hole and tied her to a stake. Overhead was a large scoop that starting piling books on top of her. When just her head was visible, a flame thrower started to set the books on fire. This scared her mother so much, she said she was sorry and her ring turned green. Both of them left the Maze and returned to their rooms.

I was still wanting to call my boyfriend, but I had no idea how to get past all the firewalls and safe guards that the domed, underwater facility had put in place. Maybe I could invent a way to communicate with the outside world, but I would have to think about it. In the meantime, I turned on the TV to see what number had been chosen for the day. The number was

43. The contestant's name was Bluebonnet. Her parents were not feeding her at home and made her wear soiled clothes to school. Her teeth were already rotten from not ever going to a dentist. Her shoes were so ugly and old that she hid a pair of old rain boots in her school locker where she could change into them while leaving her ugly shoes in the locker until the end of the day. She learned how to sew in home economics so she could design some clothes that looked like the other students'. She also found a hotel washer and dryer so she could clean her old clothes. The ring turned red, and the two contestants entered the Holodeck Maze Game. Bluebonnet chose to create a game for her mother. The room was dark and only one spot light was turned on in the middle of a stage. Her mother was dressed in dirty and torn clothes while the audience booed and hissed at her. She was allowed to try to sew a dress from scratch from a pattern that was given to her. She sat down at a sewing machine and proceeded to put together a pretty dress. It took a long time, but she finally finished. She changed into the new dress, and the audience cheered and clapped in approval. Her ring turned green because she was sorry about treating her daughter so badly and said she would see that she had only the best clothes from now on. The two left the Maze Game and returned to their rooms.

The next day I turned on the TV and saw the number 23. Her name was Lady Slipper. Her mother would take her to the bathroom when she would not do all her chores, lock the door, fill the tub with water, and hold her head under the water until she almost stopped breathing. When their rings turned red, they entered the Holodeck Maze. Lady Slipper decided to create her own game. She put her mother in a large glass cage and started to fill it up with water. Her mother tried to tread water for some time, but she finally was exhausted and began to sink under and had trouble holding her breath. The mother found the drain at the bottom of the cage and began taking it off so the water would go down the tube away from the cage. Her mother could not keep up with the water pouring into the top of the cage and started to turn blue from lack of oxygen. She sank to the bottom of the glass tank and found an oxygen tank and mask in the corner. She put it on and quickly caught her breathe. She tried to wiggle through the drain to escape. She found herself in a glass tube leading to an underground cavern where all kinds of fish were swimming. She tried to find dry land so she could pull herself out of the water before her oxygen ran low. In the cavern was a tent that had all she needed to survive a few days. There was another river that seemed to lead to a dry cave. She put on her oxygen tank and mask and tried to enter the water and try to find a way out of the cavern. She encountered all kinds of sea life and a boat that had a ladder leading up to the deck. She climbed up the ladder and found sleeping quarters below deck where she could rest awhile before she would try to steer the boat to an island that she could see through the fog. After she woke up, she set sail for the distant island. When she arrived on the sandy shore, she found a small beach house that had everything she would need in order to survive. She went to sleep, and she awoke when a loud crash occurred outside her house. There was a large animal with blue hair and a long tail trying to get into her house. There were no weapons nearby so she tried to escape by heading back to her boat. Her daughter sent her a message in a bottle that told her that all was forgiven and would she please say she was sorry. Her mother was so grateful that her ring turned green, and she told her daughter how sorry she was to have abused her. The two went arm and arm back to their rooms.

The next morning I got up early and took a swim in my pool. The television was on and announced that the next number chosen was 3. The contestant's name was Wren. He had received threats on his computer from four boys at his school. His parents had taken away his computer and closed his Facebook access. Wren chose to create his own game since there were four boys and his mother to deal with. All their rings turned red, and they all proceeded to the Holodeck maze. When they entered the Maze, they found themselves in a forest where there were all kinds of animals roaming around. They felt safe until a pack of wolves caught their scent and started tracking them. They found a tree house with a ladder which allowed all of them to take shelter. It was a good thing because the wolves chasing them were invisible werewolves with glowing eyes. The pack of wolves kept them at bay by circling the tree house. The contestants found some food and ate all they could. They then lay down on the mats on the floor and went to sleep feeling safe. The next morning they looked down to see if the wolves had gone away. There was no sign of their glowing eyes so they decided to climb down the ladder and look for safer shelter. After walking several miles, they found a larger tree house so they used the ladder to climb up and see how far they could see into the forest. There were larger trees and a mist over the mountains in the distance. Since there was more food there, they decided to spend the night. What they didn't count on was that during the night the limbs of the tree house grew larger and larger until they formed a cage around the tree house. When they woke up the next morning, they could not get out of the tree house. They tried to pull the limbs off but they wouldn't budge. Since there were no tools around, they tried to make a fire to burn a pathway through. Just as they were about to give up, a large thunder storm formed and lightning struck the side of the tree house making a hole large enough to escape. After they all climbed down to the ground, they found themselves neck deep in water. They all gave up and said they were sorry, and their rings turned green. As the contestants left the Holodeck Maze, they all hugged each other and said they would never bully anyone again. The mother said she would give Wren his computer and Facebook access as soon as they got home.

The next morning the machine chose the number 5. Her name was Quail. Her parents would take turns whipping her with a leather belt while the other one held her down. When this was reported to the police, she had bruises. The parents simply padded the belt so it would not create welts. Quail chose to create her own game. As the parent's rings turned red, they entered the Holodeck Maze. They were stripped of all their clothing and placed in a large machine that looked like a car wash. They were tightly bound to a metal pole while large brushes filled with belts whirled around their bodies until they were red and bruised from the constant whippings. Liquid was poured over them that caused the bruises to burst open into large boils. The whirling belts kept going faster and faster until the parents said they were sorry and their rings turned green. The contestants left the Maze and returned to their rooms. Their ankle bracelets that the police had put on them were flashing red and had to be readjusted.

I awoke early and had time to fix a good breakfast and swim in my pool. I still can't figure out how to reach my boyfriend. When I turned on the TV, the number chosen was 2. The name of the contestant was Willow. His mother did not give him breakfast before he left for school, and he had to stand in the snow to catch his bus. When their rings turned red, they both left for the Holodeck Maze. Willow wanted to create a game. He called it "Snow Bird". His mother was placed on a faraway planet that was made of only frozen ice. She did not have any food source until she reached the end of a long icy maze that was designed to show her how it felt to be both cold and hungry. She found the pathway hard, and she was so cold she was turning blue. Willow took pity on her and let her find a polar bear coat and boots to wear while she was searching for food. Finally, she found a large box that was full of power bars and water. She ate it all at once and said she was sorry for the abuse she had done to her son. Her ring turned green, and both contestants left the Holodeck Maze. They went back to their rooms, and the mother took a hot bath and ate a large protein meal. Willow had gained some of his weight back because he had been eating everything in the vending machine.

The next morning when I got up and turned on the TV, I saw that the number 13 had been chosen. The contestant's name was Violet. He had been adopted by a gay couple who made him work for his food by performing different sex acts with them. He was so young that when his ring turned red, and he went to the Holodeck Maze. He couldn't create a game so he chose a preprogrammed one called "Surgery". His abusers were lying on a hospital bed about to have heart surgery. The doctors walked in and put them under using an anesthetic. They feel asleep, but they could still hear and feel everything the doctors are saying and doing. They try to move, but they are paralyzed. The doctors want to use them for experiments. They hear the doctors arguing about whether or not to cut their chests open without harming their vital organs. When they start cutting into their chest wall, the pain is unbearable. The doctors remove their intestines, stomach, and liver. They cannot see their hearts well enough, so they break into the rib cage and experiment by injecting different chemicals into the heart. Then they begin injecting chemicals into the brain, causing horrible hallucination. They remove pieces of the brain to see what each piece does when it is electrically stimulated. When they finish taking notes, they put all of the organs back. They put them into a casket, and bury them alive. There is no way out of the casket, and they are running out of oxygen. Soon all of the oxygen is gone, and they are suffocating. At the last minute, the casket opens up and they are thrown into a hole where they hear growls from four lions. They are attacked when they try to run, but this fails, and the lions eat them alive. As they are dying, their rings turn green, and the game is stopped. They both ask for forgiveness and walk out of the Holodeck Maze Game. When they return to their room, they are sick at their stomachs and ask Violet to give them a second chance at being good parents. Violet says he can't return to their way of life and tells them to never see or touch him again.

The number picked by the machine today was 11. His name was Nene. His father tried to drown him when they went fishing in the ocean. The father told him he could not feed nor take care of all the five children he already had. When their rings turned red, both contestants entered the Holodeck Maze. Nene chose a preprogramed game called "Shark Attack". The father was given dive equipment and was sent to the middle of the Atlantic Ocean. He was given a spear for fishing. As the ocean pulled him farther and farther away from the shore, he panics and swims looking around for the shore. He knows that sharks come out to feed at night so he hopes he can find a way to get out of the water. Night falls, and he keeps his spear gun close by and ready to use. He turns on a flotation device on his suit to sleep, but while he sleeps, his spear gun malfunctions and shoots him in his leg. Blood gushes out of his leg and spreads through the ocean water. He fears for his life and hopes that the sharks don't smell the blood. The sun starts to rise, and he loses more blood. He finds himself in the middle of a school of jelly fish which start to sting him on his legs and back. He is attacked by an aggressive shark that bites his left leg off. The shark circles around and bites the flotation device causing all the air to be lost. His oxygen is gone in his diving gear, and he sinks into the water and begins to drown. He calls out to his son to save him and says he is sorry he tried to drown him. His ring turns green, and his son stops the game. They both walk out of the Holodeck Maze and the father vows he will try to be a better father.

The next morning I turned on the TV to see the new number that was chosen. It was number 20. The contestants name was Oriole. He was adopted by a gay father who used him for bait when he went stalking other gays at bars around town. He was then forced to give oral sex to the other gay guys. Their rings turned red, and they entered the Holodeck Maze. Oriole chose to create a game. He sent his father to a large cow farm that supplied gallons of milk to the surrounding community. A large collecting tube was attached to the back of his father's throat. He was put on a wooden slab with wheels and positioned under each cow where he had to suck the milk out of the cow's udder. After collecting milk from ten cows, the father's face turned red, and he started to throw up. He asked for forgiveness, and his ring turned green. Oriole stopped the game, and they left the Holodeck Maze. His father promised that he would never ask his son to give oral sex again.

The next number chosen was 22. Her name was Apple. She had epileptic seizures once a week, but her parents told her she was just faking it and would not take her to a doctor. Apple chose to create a game. Her parents were sent to a hospital where they were attached to an electrical device that caused them to have multiple seizures. After several hours of this treatment, they both asked for forgiveness for not listening to their daughter and promised to send her to a doctor to receive adequate treatment for her epileptic seizures. As their rings turned green, the family left the Holodeck Maze with an understanding of what they had put their daughter through.

I was glad that the game was over so quickly, and I decided to see what kind of fish were swimming outside my window. They were so beautiful and serene that I was able to go to sleep right away. The next morning I woke up and turned on the TV to see what number had been chosen. The number was 34. His name was Prairie. His father tried to teach him how to hunt deer with a bow and arrow, but when he tried to kill the deer, he cried and ran away. Prairie chose to create a game. He sent his father to a beautiful, green forest where there were many deer. Each deer had a different kind of weapon and started hunting his father. One deer shot him with an electric stun gun, and another shot him with a laser gun that knocked him out. When the father woke up, he tried to hide from the deer who were stalking him. This succeeded for a while, but the deer finally found him and begin shooting all kinds of ballistic weapons at him. The father saw that it was useless to hide and asked his son for forgiveness and that he would never ask him to kill another deer. Their rings turned green, and they left the Holodeck Maze together.

I awoke the next morning and turned on the TV. The number chosen was 36. Her name was Flycatcher. Her father had disowned her and left the family fortune to her two brothers in his will when he died. Both their rings turned red, and they entered the Holodeck Maze Game. Flycatcher chose to create her own game. She sent her father forward into the future to see how the two brothers would use their inheritance. They both invested in the stock market with most of the money, but the stock market bubble burst, and they lost all of their stock. With what little was left, they bought a house, but it went underwater during a recession, and they were out in the street with nothing. The father got so angry that he swore he would change his will and leave all of his estate to Flycatcher. His ring turned green, and both the contestants left the Holodeck Maze. He apologized to his daughter for leaving her out of his will and said he would go to his attorney immediately to make her the sole heir of his estate.

The number chosen for the next day was 42. Her name was Iris. Her mother's boyfriend told her that he was going to kill her while she slept because she would not do what he told her to do. Iris and her mother's boyfriend went to the Holodeck Maze when their rings turned red. Iris chose to create her own game. She sent the boyfriend to the top of the highest mountain and put him on a one foot ledge. As long as he was awake, he was ok, but if he went to sleep for just a second, he would fall to his death. He managed to stay awake for 24 hours, but then he started slipping off to sleep. Just as he was falling to his death, his ring turned green and the game was stopped. As they both walked out of the Holodeck Maze, he apologized to her for threatening her and said he would never do that again.

I turned on the TV, and the number for the day was 40. Her name was Jessamine. Her mother had tied her to her bed at night because she had a history of sleep walking. She had bed sores on her back from sleeping in the same position too long. As their rings turned red, the two contestants entered the Holodeck Maze. Jessamine chose to create her own game. She sent her mother back in time to a nunnery where she was being punished by being tied down on a wooden plank and not allowed to move. The nuns would throw salt water over her body twice a day to make sure the soars on her body would not get infected. The mother cried and asked for forgiveness from her daughter so Jessamine stopped the game, and their rings turned green as they left the Holodeck Maze.

The next day, number 44 was chosen. His name was Seagull. His gay father tried to make him participate in a three way sex act with two other men. When he had refused, his father locked him in his room and took away all his video games. Both of their rings turned red, and they entered the Holodeck Maze. Seagull chose a preprogrammed game called "Alone in Space". He sent his father into the future where he wakes up in a metal room. He starts to worry and looks around because he does not remember entering the room. He begins to hear strange noises coming from the far end of a long hallway. He decides to continue down the hallway, and he sees dead soldiers and blood. He finds one soldier barely alive and asks him where they are. The soldiers tells him that he is aboard a starship orbiting around a strange planet in a nearby galaxy. The soldier also tells him that there are alien monsters aboard the ship. He finds another man and asks him how to get off the ship. The soldier tells him that there is a teleportation device at the far end of the ship, but there are hundreds of alien monsters near it. He continues down the hallway and finds a monster. It charges him, and he shoots it in the head. It continues to run toward him. He shoots the monster's limbs off so it cannot run. He encounters many more monsters along the way, but he kills them by dismembering their limbs. He gets to a huge room the size of a football stadium and sees the teleportation device located down in the middle of the spaceship. He sees gas tanks that he can shoot at to kill all of the remaining monsters, but it might also damage the spaceship. He decides to shoot the gas tanks, which kills most of the monsters, but it also damages the spaceship and sends it plummeting towards a nearby planet. He runs towards the teleportation device and starts it up, but a monster grabs him and rips his legs off. He shoots it and another one appears and grabs him sending both of them out into space, which causes them to explode and die in space. The father's ring barely turned green before he died so his son stopped the game, and they both left the Holodeck Maze. His father said he was sorry for all the abuse he had caused and would never do anything to harm him again.

I thought that the game was very graphic and scary. It gave me nightmares, but I finally woke up and turned on the TV to see the next number. It was 46. Her name was American Dogwood. Her father had taken her to a local bar and made her drink five glasses of beer then laughed at her when she got dizzy and collapsed on the floor. Both their rings turned red, and they entered the Holodeck Maze. She decided to create her own game by sending her father into a large alcoholic lake without a boat and just a small life jacket. He choked on the toxic water and looked around for a place of safety that he could swim to, but there was nothing. He had no other water nor food. His body began to become water soaked by the alcohol, and raw sores began forming on his arms and legs. He cried out to his daughter that he was sorry, and he would never have her consume alcohol again. She stopped the game, and their rings both turned green. They left the Holodeck Maze arm in arm.

The next morning came quickly. I turned on the TV and saw the number 48 had been chosen. Her name was Rhododendron. She had tried to hang herself in the school after four of her classmates bullied her. She decided to create her own game for the four bullies. As all their rings turned red, they entered the Holodeck Maze. She sent them all to a bull fighting arena in Spain. She dressed all of them in red capes that went over their heads with slits just small enough to see what was happening. They were then tied upside down by their feet hanging just three feet from the sandy floor. She released ten bulls with sharp horns into the arena. They immediately starting charging the red capes. The four bullies had just enough room to swing out of the way of the sharp horns. After a few hours, the bullies lost their strength, and the bulls began to pierce them on their arms and legs. The bullies were so scared that they all asked Rhododendron to forgive them. Their rings turned green, and they all left the Holodeck Maze swearing that would never bully her again.

The number chosen the next morning was 4. Her name was Mockingbird. Her parents would starve her if she did not help clean out the chicken houses. The temperatures in the chicken houses were so hot she had to strip down to her underwear and the chickens' dropping were ankle deep. She had to pick up all the dead chickens and carry them to a nearby burning barrel. She never got breakfast before school, and she was not given any money for her school lunch. She was bullied at school because her home did not have a shower and she smelled of chicken droppings.

After school, her stepfather would beat her with a leather shaving strap if she did not complete all the evening chores which would be mopping the wooden floors and cleaning out the outhouse in her yard. She had a blood infection from a sore on the bottom of her foot which would not heal so she had to wear her older sister's shoes to school. She had two other sisters who met the same fate each day. When their rings turned red, they entered the Holodeck Maze. She decided to create her own game for her stepfather. She sent him to the future on a dark planet where giant chickens roamed. He was attacked by a flock of man eating chickens that threw him into a cesspool of chicken manure. He almost drowned as he sank to the bottom, but he managed to rise to the top of the manure and swim to a small island where he hide in a large tree until morning. When he tried to climb down the tree, the giant chickens started attacking him again. He retreated back into the tree until it got dark. When all was quiet, he managed to crawl down the tree and find refuge in a large cave that had running water in it. He cleaned himself off and started hunting for food. He carved a tree limb into a bow and found some smaller sticks that worked well as arrows. He chipped away at the walls of the cave rock and attached the sharpened stones onto the arrow heads. When morning came, he decided to go hunting in the forest. He took aim at one of the giant chickens and killed it. All he needed now was a way to start a fire. A thunderstorm poured rain and lightning all around him, and he managed to start a small fire from one of the trees that was struck with lightning.

After he ate, he looked for a way out of the forest. He got lost and fell into a large pit that was full of chicken manure. This time he could not find a way to get out and felt himself slowly drowning. He called out to his daughter to save him and that he was sorry for abusing her all those years. She stopped the game when his ring turned green, and they left the Holodeck Maze and returned to their rooms.

I thought that the game was gross, but he deserved what he got because he had been so cruel to his daughter. I went to sleep. The next morning, the number chosen was 10. Her name was Thrasher. Her mother had sliced her inner thighs with a razor blade every time she would not do her chores. As their rings turned red, they entered the Holodeck Maze. Thrasher decided to create her own game. She sent her mother back in time to France when they had just invented the guillotine. Her mother was put in jail along with other French citizens who were destined to die the next day on the guillotine. The jail was filthy and had rats running around. There was no food to eat, and she was starving. She looked around for a way to get out of the jail cell, but there was no escape. The next morning, she was put in a cart with the other prisoners and sent to the area where the guillotine was being used to chop off heads. She was the last person to be put on the chopping block. She was so afraid that she asked her daughter to forgive her. As he ring turned green, Thrasher stopped the game. They left the Holodeck Maze together. Her mother said she would never abuse her again.

The next morning, the number chosen was 14. His name was Peony. His parents assigned him to pick all the cotton on their farm before the school bus arrives. If he didn't get two bags of cotton, his parents made him walk to school which was over ten miles away, and the dirt road was full of rocks. He also had some encounters with wild wolves and bears. Their rings turned red, and they entered the Holodeck Maze. Peony decided to create his own game. He sent his father back to the Civil War time when slaves were made to pick cotton in the hot sun on southern plantations. He was given a bag that he had to fill before he was allowed to rest. The whole time, the owner had a slave handler whip the backs of all the cotton pickers to make them work harder. His father's shirt was torn by the whip, and his back was bloody and sore. After several days of this treatment, the father told his son he was sorry for abusing him. His son stopped the game when his father's ring turned green, and they left the Holodeck Maze together.

The next number chosen was 31. Her name was Roadrunner. Her father would come into her room at night and touch her private parts. She had been afraid to tell her mother, but when she did, the police put her father in jail, and he had to register as a sex offender. Both their rings turned red, and they entered the Holodeck Maze. She decided to use a preprogrammed game called "Torture" because she felt that her father was deserving of extreme punishment. The father was sent to China and was captured by the Chinese government. They think he is a spy for the

United States. They tell him to talk, but he tells them he is there for an important business meeting. The Chinese officials take out torture devices and place them in front of him. They take out pliers and pull out his fingernail. He tells them that he is not a spy so they pull out another. The pain is horrific. They pull out all of his fingernails and then pull out all of his toenails. Then they break all of his fingers and toes with a hammer. Next, they take out a power drill and drill holes into his hands and feet. He begs them to stop, but they continue. They pull out a sledge-hammer and break both of his legs. Then they break his arms and collar bone. They put him on a table and electrocute him. They cut off his fingers and saw off both of his feet. They grab a hot frying pan to cauterize the wounds to prevent him from bleeding out. They pour gasoline over his right arm and set it on fire. Then they take his left arm and pour acid on it. They continue to electrocute him until he passes out. They wait until he wakes up and repeat the torture. They pick up the sledge hammer again and smash it into his ribs, breaking his ribs and causing his ribs to deflate both of his lungs. He starts to suffocate on his own blood and just before he dies, he calls out for his daughter to stop the game because he is sorry that he had abused her. Both their rings turn green, and they leave the Holodeck Maze.

The next morning, the number chosen was 35. His name was Scarlet. His mother had given all of her attention to his little sister. When he tried to get his mother to hug him, she slapped him across the face and called him a sissy. As their rings turned red, and they entered the Holodeck Maze, his mother tried to hug him and told him that she was sorry. He accepted her apology, and he decided to forgive her. They did not have to enter the Maze. Their rings turned green, and they went back to their rooms.

I was happy that the game ended well. I was exhausted from the game before this one called "Torture". I went to bed. The next morning, I turned on the TV to see what number had been chosen. It was number 39. Her name was Island Red. Her father had teased her about being mentally retarded because she could not remember names. It turned out that she was a genius when it came to music, and she made the first chair at high school for playing the violin. When their rings turned red, they went into the Holodeck Maze. She chose to create her own game. She put her father into a large auditorium where there were many people who had come to hear her violin concert. She started to play, and the music from her violin was beautiful. After rounds of applause, she was given a standing ovation. Her father realized how much he had misjudged her and asked to be forgiven. His ring turned green, and they left the Holodeck Maze together.

The next number chosen was 1. His name was Yellow-hammer. He had heard some of his classmates talking about how they were going to hurt another student. The rings turned red and Yellow-hammer and the four classmates entered the Holodeck Maze. Yellow-hammer chose to create a game for the four bullies. He placed them into a volcano where they would have to find a way to escape the molten lava. They were hot and choking from all the fumes. When they started trying to find a way out, the walls started crumbling and falling down around them. They heard a loud voice warning them that they were in danger of dying from the heat. This scared them so much that they asked for forgiveness. Their rings turned green, and they left the Holodeck Maze and returned to their rooms vowing that they would never plot to hurt any other students in their school.

HOLODECK GAMES OVER

It was announced that the Holodeck Maze Games were over. The abusers were asked to leave their rooms, pick up their one million dollar checks for their participation, and return to the airport to fly home. Their angel rings were removed.

The children who were abused were given the choice of returning with their parents or flying to their new homes with their million dollar checks. It was left entirely up to them as to what they wanted to do. Most of the contestants chose to go to their new homes, but a few decided to return with their parents. A follow up explaining how each child felt after they observed what each of their parents experienced going through the games that had been picked for them would be mailed in to the main control center at a later date.

The future was bright for the abused children because they not only got to force their abusers to say they were sorry, but their every wish would come true when they started their new life. Their angel rings turned into golden diamond rings which were easily removed. I just then realized that my name and my mother's did not come up so I decided to go home with her and be grateful that my life was so good! Plus, I would get to tell my boyfriend about all my adventures!

Printed in the United States
By Bookmasters

ADULT HUNT

An exciting science-fiction story that helps abused children know they are not alone and where they may go for help. They create or choose Holodeck Maze Games that their abusers must go through until they show remorse for their actions. At that point, their angel rings' eyes turn from red to green, and they get to leave the game and return to their room. In the end, the children get to choose where they will live. The parents return home. Both are a million dollars richer for their participation.

Dr. Roselinda Johnson, Ed.D., spent twenty years in education and fifteen years as a licensed professional counselor. During this time, she documented many clients' stories of abuses that they were subjected to by their parents, friends, or strangers. The children did not know where to go for help. Dr. Johnson wrote this book as a tribute to these children, who are protected with code names that are the symbols of each of the fifty states included in Book 1 Gathering of Contestants for the Holodeck Maze Games. Book 2 shows which type of Holodeck Maze Game each child chose to punish their abusers until they showed remorse or until their rings turned back to green.

ISBN 978-1-5049-1954-8

authorHOUSE®

What
I Do
Know Is...

The Truth as I Know It

Sherrie Raquel